CW00421400

I Don't Want To G
To School Today

By Nix Henderson

Written for Archie Henderson

A note for readers - name of child, teachers and friends can be

substituted in order to personalise the story

Illustrated by Perry-May Britton

Published by Emma & Charlotte Henderson

May 2022

"I don't want to go to school today" sighed Archie, as he climbed into his Mummy and Daddy's bed for a morning cuddle. "Why ever not?" replied Mummy sleepily. "I don't feel well and I'm sooo tired and it's raining- I'm not going to school today."

Mummy sat herself up, and put her arm around Archie.

"Oh Archie, if you didn't go to school today, you would be

missed sooooo much...." Archie looked inquisitive. "Well,"

sighed Mummy snuggling Archie even closer to her,

"everyone would sit down for the register and when your teacher called out your name... there would be a gasp as your friends realised you weren't here today.

Ed, Peter, Jamie, Josh and Matthew would all start crying and crying... "Who will we play with?" they all tremored.

And then your special helpers and your teachers would begin to sob too, until everyone in Pear Class would be making such noise, that somebody from the next door classroom might come in and ask what all the noise was about.

"Archie isn't here today" your teacher would explain and "We are all so sad." Soon, as each class realised that Archie was not at school, every child and every teacher began to wail and cry, snuffling could be heard everywhere.

When the office ladies heard, they too started to cry.
They made such a loud noise and there was so much
crying going on, that the Headmaster came out to see
what all the terrible commotion was about.

There were so many tears, that by now a steady trickle of water could be seen seeping out of each classroom, quickly joining the river of salty tears running down the school corridors.

Book bags and water bottles could be seen bobbing up
and down, books, plimsolls and pencils joined the
surging waters.

Nobody could be consoled, and soon the playground began
to fill up too...

"Oh no there is a flood of tears rising across the whole school....and all because Archie isn't here today." Yelled the Headmaster...

"We must call the Police!"

And so....the office ladies kindly called The Police and explained what was going on.

The Police decided that the only thing was to go and fetch

Archie and bring him into school.

Rat a tat tat, went the door knocker at Archie's house

"Good morning Archie" said the Policemen softly...

And he gently explained that everyone at school was
crying so hard because they were missing Archie; "As you
are obviously so special, would you and your Mummy like
to come in my police car?"

They drove back to the sobbing crowd of friends and teachers. They turned on the blue flashing siren light- because after all this was an emergency....

And they got there just in time to prevent the whole village from flooding!

Everyone clapped and cheered...

and at last the school day could begin!

"And so" Mummy said, "We really wouldn't want all that
to happen would we?

And besides there wouldn't be enough tissues and it
would take days for the school to dry out."

Archie smiled, slipped out of bed and a few minutes later was looking so smart and handsome in his blue school uniform.

"Come on Mummy-get up! we better get a move on!"

THE END

"I Don't Want To Go To School Today" was written by Nix Henderson back in 2011 when her 8 year old son Archie kept telling her "I don't want to go to school today".

Nix sadly passed away the following year in May 2012. Nix left behind her children Charlotte (now 24), Emma (now 22), Archie (now 19), and her husband and father to her children, Andy. Nix's youngest daughter Emma, found this story saved on her laptop years later and has decided to publish it to celebrate and remember her mum, 10 years on from her death and as a gift to Archie for his 18th birthday.

This book has been brilliantly illustrated by Perry-May Britton who was Nix's best friend. They met in Harare (Zimbabwe) as teenagers and continued their friendship through university in Cape Town (South Africa), young adult life in London (England) and then family life in Sussex (England). Perry-May is a gifted illustrator and close friend of the Hendersons. Emma knew she wanted Perry-May to illustrate the book because she knew Nix would have asked her to, and here it is!

A word from Emma - "This book is incredibly special to my family and to anyone who knew my mum, as you can quite literally hear her in it. She was the most amazing mum; full of fun, care, a good dose of silliness and more love than we could have ever hoped for or desired. We miss her everyday but we are so proud of how we're getting on without her. She made me and my siblings who we are today and for that she will never be forgotten. Thank you for taking an interest in my mum's brilliant little book, I am well aware this isn't anything groundbreaking (sorry mum!) but it is full of love. Someone once told me, Nix had said to them when they were pregnant *'just shower them with love, that's all kids really need!'* and she certainly did."

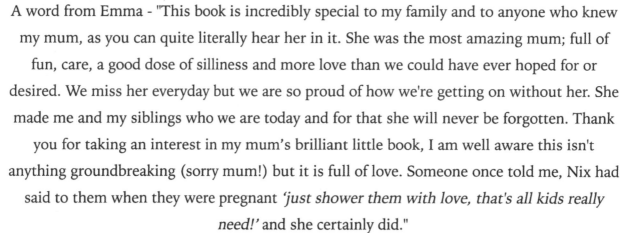

Archie, Emma & Charlotte (2021)

Nix

Emma, Archie & Charlotte (2007)

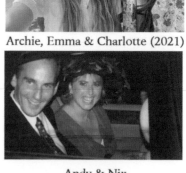

Andy & Nix

Printed in Great Britain
by Amazon